J. Wilson McLaren

Scots Poems and Ballants

J. Wilson McLaren

Scots Poems and Ballants

ISBN/EAN: 9783743307391

Manufactured in Europe, USA, Canada, Australia, Japa

Cover: Foto ©Andreas Hilbeck / pixelio.de

Manufactured and distributed by brebook publishing software
(www.brebook.com)

J. Wilson McLaren

Scots Poems and Ballants

Scots Poems

AND

Ballants

BY

J. WILSON M'LAREN

Author of " Rhymes frae the Chimla-Lug,"
" Tommy Catchiron," etc.

AT EDINBVRGH
IMPRINTED BY THE AUTHOR
177 DALKEITH ROAD
MDCCCXCII

TO BRITHER SCOTS
THE WORLD O'ER.

A Scot here endeavours to depict only that which is true to nature. His earnest desire is to be homely and natural; to touch a tender chord that may awaken the susceptibilities to a more ennobling state, or with a gleam of humour demolish the cobwebs of Melancholia from the mind.

CONTENTS.

CONTENTS.

The die is cast !   With trembling fear
  I scan the printed pages now,
  While Care still hovers on my brow,
And click of type rings in my ear.

I see the Press frail and antique,—
  And troublesome,—a dwarf in size ;
  Yet soon I learn'd to love and prize
At midnight's hour its cheery creak !

Its compass only would give birth
  And slowly, to one little page,
  But Pleasure is a golden wage,
And I had faith in hearts on earth.

Love's labour lost ?   Avaunt, grim Dread !
  From all things simple yet sincere,
  Good still may wing its flight, and rear
On barren soil a pyramid.

SCOTS POEMS AND BALLANTS.

THE PRINTING PRESS.

" Let light be."

GOD speed the craft whose potent power
   Inthralls the world to-day;
And tho' brain-rack'd hour after hour,
   We only Life's part play;
Yet what a part! let glib-tongued voice
   Deride the " art" at will;
But we as craftsmen may rejoice
   O'er no unworthy skill.

Mark Learning at the garner'd fruits!—
   While Rank and Wealth stand near—
Of those whose hearts in their pursuits
   On every page is clear!
Who fed the mind—altho' assail'd—
   With floods of heavenly light,
When venom'd Bigotry prevail'd,
   And all was dark as night!

Then let us humbly bow the head,
   And stand with bated breath,
When Fame's emblazon'd scroll is read
   And "names that know not death !"
Behold our Masters foremost placed !
   And rightly so, for they
Foul fantasies from men's hearts chased,
   And Truth held glorious sway !

The world moves on ! Great changes come,
   Until our power's ten-fold ;
But tho' the Press of old be dumb,
   No purer is the gold !
Now pulse of engines ever beat,
   The ground throbs where we stand,
And cylinders clank ! God ! what a treat
   Is modern printing-land !

Lo ! look ! the paper that was dead,
   Hath life in every vein ;
And laughter round the hearth is shed,
   Where sadness once did reign !
The greatest thoughts of master-minds,
   Thus scatter'd far and wide,
Wields moral power, and closer binds
   All nations to our side !

What of our sires begrimed and worn,
   Whose sweat-drops dyed the brow?
Oh! million millions yet unborn,
   I charge you ne'er allow
Oblivion to cast its shroud
   Around their honour'd names,
For Genius hath to them endow'd
   Imperishable claims!

—o—

A GODLY BALLANT.
MARK xii. 41-44.

THE auld kirk bells were jowlin' lood,
   An' thrang was the hie an' laigh road,
Wi' haly folk an' hypocrites,
   On their way to the hoose o' God.

The Maister at the kirk-yett stuid,
   As a laird wi' his heid fu' hie,
In gangin' by drapt in the plate
   What he could weel afford to gie.

An' mony mair cam' stappin' in,
   But oh, in heart thae werena' true,
Yet that gied them fu' little thocht,
   For grand were thae in ootward view.

Syne in a widow hirplin' cam',
  Wha was righteous in heart tho' puir,
An' put a farden canny doon—
  'Twas a' the auld body could spare.

The Maister's een were wat wi' tears
  As he turn'd to the Twal' an' said—
" Mark'd ye the walthy carles wha
  Mak' liberality a trade;

An' this puir wifie? she has gien
  Far mair to God's service than a'
This day, for oh, her heart was true
  In the gie'in' o' it awa!"

.   .   .   .

Ay, e'en to this day ye will find monie folk—
  Their sauls black wi' vice, whyles in fear
To God's hoose repair in hypocrisy's cloak,
  An' wi' aumus their conscience wad clear!

But priceless the dower in Death's fell glamourie,
  Whilk in scripture like this somehow rins—
Respecter o' persons God never can be,
  An' gowd winna blot oot oor sins!

STANZAS ANENT A CUDGEL.

PRESERVE us ! what a muckle stick !
'Twad tak' the breath e'en frae Auld Nick !
Or better still some Home Rule Mick,
          Help in debate ;
For chiels wi' it wha got a lick,
            Wad soon be quate !

When I, fu prood, the stick produced,
My mither vow'd she wadna' hoose't,—
An' waur, I'd in the bine be soused,
          Gin I'd no burn it !
I'se half inclined frae words she used,
          Then to return it !

But courage ! quick I to the flare,
An' dang the leg clean aff a chair !
Waesucks ! she could do nocht but stare,
          Wi' hands aloft,
An' cry, "My conscience ! Jock, tak' care !
          Ye're surely dauft !"

"Dauft ? far frae that," I made reply,
As, swish ! three mair legs gaed awry ;

" There! that's a proof ye needna' try
                    To put me past it ;
Frae oot the hoose, tho' sair ye cry,
                    I ne'er will cast it !"

Losh keep's ! gin my respectit mither,
Had got the hale length o' her tether,
The keepsakes folk gie ane anither
                    At antrin times,
She'd sweep frae sicht withoot a swither
                    Like my puir rhymes !

Richt fervently I've often prayed
That when my part in life is played,
This stick will be 'neath nae glass shade,
                    But ever ready
For some frien' wha micht need its aid,
                    Wi' steps unsteady.

—o—

A SCOT ABROAD.

'Tis meet that we should sit within our room
    Alone, to-night, in sweetest reverie,
    And let our thoughts be wafted o'er the sea,
And break the year's dull, melancholy gloom.

Yet why be sad? June, with its balmy breath,
  Draws fragrance sweet from every budding flower,
  So let us now but consecrate an hour,
And from the Past weave Bygones as from death!

Alive—yet dead! for in that distant clime
  His voice is heard not, nor his smiling face
  Is with us now the homely hearth to grace,
As in our childhood's joyous summer-time.

So, on his natal day, 'tis fitly we,
  As Scots, remembrance prove for auld langsyne,
  And toast his worth, that ne'er with us will tine—
God's grace, good health, and fair prosperity!

May such be his: and when Life's cherished prize
  In after years he holds in faithful trust;
  Youth, battling on, with hope will look, and must
As from the mountain spring refreshed arise!

As lovers yearn when Fate keeps them apart,
  Thus we to-night must drop a silent tear,
  For with our hope there always comes the fear;
So, brother, take this song-gift from the heart!

—o—

GREYFRIARS BOBBY.

A DOWG'S APPEAL TO THE PROVOST, BAILIES, COUNCILLORS, AND CITIZENS O' AULD REEKIE.

At a meeting of the Edinburgh Town Council on February 5th 1889, a letter was read from Archibald Langwill, C. A., which stated that a movement was some time ago set on foot to collect subscriptions from children with the view of perpetuating the memory of the dog known as "Greyfriars Bobby" by erecting a monument in Greyfriars Churchyard. Several hundreds of children gladly subscribed, and on their behalf he asked permission to do so. Councillor Gillies, in reply said that the story of " Greyfriars Bobby " was a penny-a-liner's romance. There was no truth in it at all. "Greyfriars Bobby" had no beloved master, and was just a mongrel of the High Street breed.

*" We have some satisfaction to-day in applying correction to a serious act of injustice done to an old Edinburgh favourite. In his haste at the Town Council meeting, Councillor Gillies said that the romantic story of 'Greyfriars Bobby' was all humbug, and that its fame was got on false pretences. According to Mr Gillies, ' Bobby ' was a very ordinary cur indeed—a mere High Street wastral. Not a single Councillor had patriotic sentiment or spirit enough to raise a word of protest ; they were all as dumb dogs. It will create no surprise if at the next meeting an attempt be made to prove that Wallace and Bruce, were mythical personages. The romance of 'Greyfriars Bobby' is no myth."—*EVENING DISPATCH.

WHAUR is the dowg that bears a name,
That winna hand his heid wi' shame?

Since that bauld billie in the Chaumer—
Wi' meikle o' an auld wife's yammer,
Has taen the task upon himsel',
To break the sweet romantic spell ;
To delve in history o' the past,
And now proclaim to east and wast,
To north and south, that Greyfriars Bobby,
Is just a myth—a hearsay hobby ;
In fact, to gie a dowg a bad name,
Wha only what is truthfu' wad claim.

  It looks as if some civic chiels,
Were mair than anxious for the "seals,"
For like some dowgs that I could mention,
Thae daily bark to draw attention ;
And tho' chasteezed, like some puir messin,
Thae aye forget the painfu' lesson !
Or why this idle controversy,
And on a dowg that's at their mercy ?

  The "laughter," and the cries "Hear, hear,"
A' this and mair I weel can bear,
But when thae wander frae the truth,
I canna sit and haud my mooth !

  "A mongrel o' the High Street breed !"
Is language far owre strong, indeed ;
It ill befits the chiel wha said it,

And folk wha live there has degraded.
Now in their minds they'll hae to bear,
That South Side villas thae maun rear,
And be like Councillors, snug and crouse,
Wi' grund at front and back o' hoose!
  Tho' for mysel', I maun confess,
I like the High Street nane the less,
For what langsyne was there enactit,
When women young and auld distractit,
View'd Scotland's sons wi' hope 'gae 'wa,
But doom'd on Flodden sune to fa'!
Or when the charger, weary worn,
Wha frae the fecht had Murray borne,
Wi' clattering hoofs forth a' did bring,
To hear the fate o' Scotland's King!
Or later still, when ladies fair,
And men chivalrous welcom'd there,
Wi' roses white that charm'd ilk e'e,
Prince Charlie, fresh frae victory!
But words o' mine are little needit,
When in Scots history a' can read it.
  Is there a patriotic soul,
Sae base as now its doonfa' thole,
And cast sic slurs wi' pompous air,
When poortith's load's eneuch to bear?

But cringe I'll no, nor hing my tail,
When Ignorance wad thus assail;
And tho' my lines I haena got
This mak's me nane the less a Scot!

I maun admit it's no in keeping,
That I wi' Martyrs should be sleeping,
Tho' often I hae gaed to view
The tomb that tells o' men sae true:
The martyr'd Marquis!—Guthrie, brave!
And Renwick, wha wad be nae slave!
Wi' ithers o' the fearless deid
Wha for the King had little dreid,
But focht against tyrannic laws,
For God,—their conscience, and a cause!
And prov'd Christ's Crown and Covenant,
To be nae idle reel-rall rant.

Wi' a' due honour to ilk bairn,
I'm no in favour o' a cairn,
Altho' waur things hae been erectit,
To show how weel the deid's respectit!
(Oor auld kirkyards a wheen can boast noo,
And keepit at the public cost, too);
While tributes oft inscribed thereon,
Hae gar'd oor antiquarians groan,
For weel thae ken the best ot's fiction,

And still they're rais'd withoot restriction ;
On mony a rather doubtfu' story
We've built the best o' Scotland's glory !

I've long supplied a needfu' want,
Whilk e'en oor Council winna grant ;
When frae the Meadows folks returnin',
And wi' the summer sun are burnin'—
Or when wi' gowff, the quoits, or cricket,
Or e'en wi' Socialists been licket—
Wee Bobby, feth, is aye frequented,
And a' gang blythely aff contented ;
If only this, and naething mair,
A blessing I hae been, I'm sure.

When no lang whalpit, near St Giles,
Wi' twa three mair I rompit whiles,
But little ettled my guid name,
Wad there some day be brocht to shame.
I watched, too, chiels free o' pretence—
Wha aye spak' truth and common-sense,
Gae linkin' by in furthy crack—
Wha e'en straik't *mongrels* on the back !
And tho' a dowg I maun confess
I glowered wi' interest nane the less !
But there was ane whase honour'd name,
In a' Scots hearts has found a hame ;

A frien' to High Street dowgs was he—
It matter'd nae their pedigree,
Baith rich and poor he aye respec'it ;
In fact, mysel' wi' collar deckit !

Hech surse the day ! when dowgs protection
Are forced to claim frae foul dissection,
When things o' far mair consequence,
That baith oorsels and toon wad mense,
Are now ignored, while " archers wine, "
And sic like fads are i' the line.
The public guid ! alack a day !
Whan useless clatter hauds the sway !
Wi' sma'er rents and hooses better
Auld Reekie folks wad be their debtor ;
But progress !— no, nor e'en attention
To mony things that I could mention—
The streets, or there's the gas we're burnin',
Sae poor that some to " dips " are turnin' ;
Wi' jobbery baith richt and left,
O' sense fu' sune we'll be bereft ;
Nae wonder whiles my een I'm dichtin',
When sic as this needs sae much richtin',
It maks folk say when they're electit
Thae carena then tho' a's neglectit.
By Granny Gray's auld tirlin' pin,

I wadna be within their shoon,
But still remain a " mongrel " dowg
Wi' power to cock my tail or lug.

Had " Rab's " auld frien' been to the fore,
Wha penn'd the touching Howgate lore—
A story whaur a dowg play'd part,
That oft has moved the hardest heart,
And withoot whilk there's nane daur say
But we'd been poorer, far, the day.
To John nane ere tried to maintain
That I had sat there for a bane ;
But just to prove that dowgs whiles ken,
When richtly treated now and then,
And show to mony a bairn a lesson,
That ere thae dee may be a blessin' !

—()—

WHITE HEATHER.

CHORUS.

My heart's fu' o' joy, tho' a tear dims ilk e'e,
For, oh, visions sweet come frae yont the braid sea ;
A sprig o' white heather this nicht wafts me there ;
White heather ! white heather, I'll tend ye wi' care !

White heather frae Scotia ! my heart throbs wi' pride,
And so I will cherish't as lover his bride,
For life's sweetest treasure I won, leal and true,
Ae nicht in the gloaming whare white heather grew.

How pleasant life's spring-time—to speil the hills hie,
Whare nocht but white heather aroon ye could see,
Or sit by the burnie awa' doon the glen,
And dream o' a lassie like far aulder men.

A sprig o' white heather I brocht Ailie Broun
The nicht that we parted wi' hearts broken doon ;
The same in return, but entwined wi' her hair,
I got frae the lassie I'll never see mair !

As shadows o' eventide owre my path fa',
I sigh for the wild mountain hame far awa',
For, oh, it is there now I fain would repose
Wi' my ain kith and kin whare the white heather grows!

—o—

HENRY IRVING.

LYCEUM THEATRE, EDINBURGH, 1888.

MASTER! may time fall lightly on thy head,
    For such as thou this earth would miss full sore.
Thy great creations—which have nightly fed
    So many minds, even o'er th' Atlantic's roar—
    And others which may yet come from thy store,
Must be a priceless boon, a life's elixir which,
When thirsting youth partakes, 'twill more than gold
    enrich!
Devil thou art! but if the Reigning Power
    In Hell's abyss were privileged to view
His antitype for only one brief hour,
    Remorse, so keen, might pierce his conscience thro',
    And half the world would feel as born anew,
For this thy mission is. May God sustain thy heart
To play upon Life's stage this now much-needed part!

TIBBIE.

CHORUS.

Hech ay! oh, dearie me!
For a drap o' the nappy what wadna Tib gie;
My girnin' auld Aunty,
Whase siller is scanty,
Maun aye hae a cinder at nicht in her tea!

I HAE an auld Aunty ayont Wuddislee,
She's cock o' the midden tho' blin' o' an e'e,
  An' tak's sic delight in
  Baith girnin' an' flytin',
That a' in the clachan afore her will flee!

On the croon o' her pow there's a big plaster patch,
But losh! tak' guid care that her e'e doesna catch
  You glowerin' at her—
  Your nerves she'd sune shatter,
A tongue deavin' randie, you'll no find her match!

It's seldom that Tibbie's withoot twa black een,—
It's Johnnie Maut's trade-mark! she cares na a preen;
  Oor deacon Tam Miller,
  Ance tried to preach till her,
And for a month after't in kirk wasna seen!

The longer folk live the mair ferlies they see,
An' tho' Aunty Tib is for weeks on the spree,
  To turn owre a new leaf,
  An' end a' this sair grief,
E'er neist Hallow Fair she has promised to me!

—0—

A FALLEN ONE DEAD!

A FALLEN one dead! Yes, her short race is run,
 The wan face betrays the sad life she has led;
No sister to aid her—to pray for her—none!
 But her death-stiffened limbs and her weary head
Lie there—on the earth 'neath a cold wintry sun,
 That shines on the wreck of a beauty that's fled,
But she heeds not the shame, nor the deed that is done—
   A fallen one dead!

Alas! there are others, as this fallen one—
 In the city's foul dens where no solace is shed;
Oh, Christians! think of the creatures you shun,
 In hovels and hells, where rank infamy's fed,
There's work for redemption that's not yet begun—
 Where Christ sends His angels, ye also may tread—
And do noble duty, ah! thus left undone—
   A fallen one dead!

THE LASS O' LOGAN LEE.

THE sun owre Dun-edin was shining fu' bonnie,
    As I, and my Jeannie, strayed roun' the Braid Hills;
The lassie wi' looks more bewitching than onie,
    Whose voice is far sweeter than murmuring rills;
The mavis was warbling his wood-notes so cheery,
    And wakening the echoes o' Nature's sweet lyre,
As down on the brae-side I sat wi' my dearie,
    Enraptured wi' songs o' the wild feathered choir.

The hum o' the bees, and the kye loudly roaring,
    Brought back to our memory childhood again;
While mild summer zephyrs, tired Nature restoring,
    Flushed Jeannie's fair cheeks like the rose after rain.
A flower is my lassie, both precious and tender—
    As spotless and pure as the primrose in spring;
For beauty and wealth lordlings seek the ha's splendour,
    But when wi' my Jeannie I envy nae king.

How sweet is the 'oor wi' your love in the gloaming,
    Where meanders the burnie, or down pours the linn;
Where monie for harebell and foxglove gang roaming,
    Awa' in the country frae Labour's loud din.

Then, oh, may the Powers wha bestow on us pleasures
    That poor o' the land like the rich aye can pree,
Guard winsome young Jeannie, first o' my heart's trea-
        sures,
    Wha dwells in seclusion near sweet Logan Lee.

—o—

MIST.

I STRAYED where wild flowers wet with dew
        By mortal feet were prest,
        While o'er the Pentland's breast
Descending mist obscured the view,
And there it hung with dismal frown,
        Until the sun-god smote
        Its density afloat—
And swept the mist athwart the town.

With dusky mantle it embraced
        The towering city spires
        That paled like beacon fires,
Quenched in it s wide and humid waste;
Thus sorrow clouds the brow of man,
        And wraps his soul in gloom,
        Till hope bids joy illume
Creation's universal plan.

SHOUGGIE SHOU, MY BAIRNIE.

A MITHER'S SANG.

CHORUS.

Shouggie shou, shouggie shou !
Hush-a-ba my dearie ;
Hech surse ! but a waukrife bairn
Aye mak's a mither weary !

SHOUGGIE shou, my bairnie,
   Hush ! my bonnie doo ;
Wha sae like your ain sel' ?
   Sonnie, keekie boo !

Eenie, fegs ! ye winna close ;
   Wirr-a-wirr-a-wae !
Tak' the rattle ; that's it noo !
   Or wi' pussy play.

There's the boo-man i' the stair,
   Wi' the muckle pock ;
Steek your een ! cuddle close,
   And the door I'll lock !

Losh ! but ye're a waukrife bairn—
   Shouggie, shouggie shou !
Here, big dowgie, come ye ben,—
   Tak' him in your mou' !

Bless the lamb, he's noo asleep,
   Soun' as soun' can be ;
Noo the hearthstane I maun wash,
   Syne mak' daddie's tea !

—o—

OH, WAES ME !

I'M wae to think that poortith's load sae mony hae to
    bear—
For, oh, the reflex o' the mind is oft found in a tear ;
But courage ! tho' affliction's rife, for wha hae least to dree
Are aye the first to prostrate fa' and cry oot—" Oh, waes
    me ! "

Some folk ye'll find the hale year roun' enshrouded aye
    in gloom,
Wha speak o' hardships draggin' them to an owre early
    tomb :

Gin they wad tread life's staney road wi' hope in ilka e'e,
They'd aiblins hae fu' little cause to cry oot—" Oh, waes
me ! "

Mak' Common-sense the finger post this warld to guide
ye thro',
'Twill prove e'er lang 'tis folly to sit doon and sairly rue
The ill that's dune, or what has dimm'd at times the
wifie's e'e :
Up wi' a will ! there's prospects bricht, and cry na—" Oh,
waes me ! "

Then let us strive frae morn till mirk to fecht against
what's wrang ;
Advice and solace is required whatever road we gang ;
We're sure to be rewarded sune, then great the joy will
be ;
It's neither manly nor yet wise to cry oot—" Oh, waes
me ! "

—( )—

TO ALFRED, LORD TENNYSON.

ON READING "DEMETER AND OTHER POEMS."

To thee, whose heart is like a golden mine—
    Rich in its wealth as all may well conceive ;
This tribute to thy worth, O bard divine,
    I know thou wilt in kindly mood receive.
Tho' not with thy Promethean spirit fraught,
    For thus thy verse is nerved—intense and grand !
    Whilst its impassioned ardour stirs the land,
And vibrates in all hearts, where it has taught
    Life's deathless precepts, which I ever strive to keep ;
And trust that He to whom we humbly bend
May give thee strength to be man's truest friend !
    And in the good thou sowest may thou also reap ;
Whilst in the fervour of my heartfelt love I pray
Thy genius long may add its lustre to our day.

—o—

LADYE REA.

A BALLAD.

'Twas a cauld, cauld, an' a mirky night,
    An' the hinmost o' the year ;
The sea to the sky row'd mountains high,
    An' the forest sough'd fu' drear.

An' oh, but the thunder sounded loud,
　An' the rain rain'd heavilie;
But, hark! a wail that might a' hearts quail—
　" Whare, whare can my true luve be ? "

'Twas Ladye Rea that gaz'd on the sea,
　An' wow! but she look'd fu' braw,
As there she stood in despairing mood,
　An' aye on her luve did ca'.

Nae heed took she o' the light'ning's flash,
　Nor the rain so heavilie,
But wi' waefu' mein an' tearfu' een,
　Sobb'd—" Whare can my true luve be ? "

A sea-maw perch'd on a cliff near hand,
　Wail'd thae words mournfullie—
" Ladye, ladye fair, greet thou nae mair,
　But list what I tell to thee—

You braw sailor lad thou lo'ed so weel,
　Fause, fause has prov'd to thee,
An' taen a bride, an' gane to abide
　Awa' in a far countrie! "

" Why, an' oh why, have ye prov'd so fause,
　Oh! Leslie, come tell to me ? "

She spak' in vain, for never again
    On earth her luve she would see!

"An' now, fare thee weel," the weird maw cried,
    As it took a seaward flight,
" It's down i' the deep e'er long ye'll sleep,
    Ay, even this vera night!"

Walie! an' wae! but the maw sang true,
    For e'er that wild night had gane,
The ladye fair wi' the gowden hair
    Slept soun' i' the raging main!

    *   *   *   *   *

When the morning dawn'd wi' red-wat een,
    The laird rade oot frae the ha',
For the silence there he ill could bear;
    Her voice answered no his ca'!

An' as he rade no ae word spak' he,
    But his face his grief betray'd;
An' stalworth men frae hillside an' glen,
    A' vow'd thae would find the maid!

Thae socht her down by the birken shaw,
    Near to her stately dwellin'.

Whare oft she stray'd an' fondly play'd
   Wi' fause young Lord Dunellin.

But for 'oors in vain, tho' hearts were stirr'd,
   An' fleet o' limb were thae ;
Owre rock an' scaur, ay, even as far
   As the dreaded Martyr's Brae !

Thae found her at last upon the beach,
   The wild waves lashing o'er her ;
While her father's heart wi' woe did smart,
   For well he did adore her !

Thae howkit a grave i' the auld kirkyard,
   An' buried twa on the morrow ;
An' far, far aroun' was heard the soun'
   O' meikle dule an' sorrow !

—0—

A SUMMER-DAY DREAM.

" From Nature up to Nature's God."

ABOVE, a canopy of blue,
　　While gowans with their hearts of gold
My wayward steps to-day bestrew,
　　And mirrors back the days of old.

Life unalloyed! as virgin sweet
　　I lived and envied not the Great;
But now a slave to toil; 'tis meet
　　My soul rebels against such fate.

For freedom, yearn I ever must,
　　When earth's sweet breath around me play;
And like my forebears in the dust,
　　A wanderer wild I feel to-day.

The trembling wind, the laverock's lay,
　　The scented briar, and stretch of green,
Full regal homage needs must pay,
　　And browsing kine enhance the scene.

O God! for such an hour as this,
　　My faith in Thee is firmer set,
Tho' soured heart sapped with thoughtlessness,
　　Thy statutes haply may forget.

A SCREED TO HUGH HALIBURTON.

HETH! Hughie, man, your Ochil lays,
Like purple heather frae the braes,
Reca' to mind the langsyne days,
      An' sets me thinkin',
An' sae this nicht I maun your praise
      In rhyme be clinkin'.

For sic as I, born in the toon,
Wi' nocht but stane an' brick piled roun',
Fu' sairly miss the cheery soun'
      O' ploomen whustlin';
Or burns in spate, whyles tumblin' doon,
      An' bourtrees rustlin'.

I've Blackford Hill, an' furzy Braid,
Whare gowfer gangs, an' sickly maid;
But folk wha buckle to a trade
      Sae tight are tied, man,
That doctors thrive; for Nature's aid
      They are denied, man!

Ilk blab o' rhymin' wark's revealin'
The fact that hills ye're early speilin',
Or owre the muir at nicht whyles stealin',
    Some lass to woo ;
Syne at the shrine o' Beauty kneelin',
    Baith leal an' true!

When cronies at the smiddy gather,
To argie-bargie 'bout the weather,
Or owre some plooin' match to blether,
    I doubtna, Hugh,
Your arguments they'd whyles fain tether,
    Sae deep the view.

An' when it's wat, wi' soople rod
Ye'll seek the burn, fu' tightly shod,
Or spend a nicht attoure the brod,
    Or in the howff,
Discussing craps an' lassies snod,
    Ye'll ne'er be dowff.

An' when the win's sae awesome soughin',
Ye're, aiblins, at a rockin' hoochin',
An' hoastin' sair at times wi' leughin'
    Gin some hind tell
Hoo he ae nicht a dirty sheugh in,
    No kennin' fell!

Syne some ane else a tale may raise,
When Scots heroic met the faes ;
Their victories an' a' their waes—
   A wond'rous story,
To hear rehears'd reca' the days
    Owre whilk I glory!

For sires o' mine at fatefu' Flodden,
Wha rather than be aye doon-trodden,
Stood by their king, on ground bluid-sodden,
   That waefu' morn
The Scots, faith in their James aye hauden',
    O' life were shorn !

Sae, Hughie, wad ye deem it richt
That bard like you I'd haud fu' licht,
Wha never yet did Scotland slicht,
   But love an' honour,
In ilka grand poetic flicht
    Ye fling upon her!

Then ill befa' me for neglect
To show ere this my deep respect,
Or sowth a sang wi' guid effect
   An' roosin' chorus,
An' pray Scots hearts may ne'er be sneck't
    To " Homespun Horace ! "

THE WA-GAUN O' THE WEAN.

'Tis summer again, and the blue-bells in bloom,
A mother's heart cheers like sun piercing the gloom,
As she stands in the kirkyard beside a sma' grave,
Where they laid her wee Johnnie, along wi' the lave.

And as she looks doon wi' the tears in her een,
Wee Johnnie, before her fu' plainly is seen !
And his words aye sae pawky, like melody sweet,
Seem to float thro' the air, and she canna but greet.

A towmont has gane, but affection still keeps
His memory green, like the grave where he sleeps ;
And the gowans he loved in the spring-time to pu',
Frae the howe are transplanted and wave owre him noo.

'Twas the deid 'oor o' nicht when the angel cam' doon,
Wi' joy everlasting, Wee Johnnie, to croon,
And tho' he had suffered for weeks unco sair,
She thocht that the Lord her wee treasure would spare.

But it wasna God's will : in the auld-farrant face,
As he sat up in bed a' could Paradise trace ;

For shadows o' death like dark clouds roun' ilk e'e,
Had gather'd, and oh, it was waefu' to see.

In a voice faint and low for his father he socht,
And John to the bed-side grief-stricken they brocht;
Syne bending to catch what the wean had to say,
That night the best part in his life he did play.

Few words 'tween them pass'd, but the hand cauld as snaw,
And the blae lips wi' kisses again seem'd to thaw,
While the glisk o' a smile sune displaced the wild stare,
Ere he fell on the pillow and spak' nevermair.

When a' in the hoose, later on, sleepit soun',
The mother to where Johnnie lay, slippit doon,
And as she there stood and oft kiss'd the cauld cheek,
Sae life-like he look'd that she thocht he would speak.

Fu' lanesome and dreary that day was their hame,
Tho' mony folk gaed, ay, and mony folk came;
But few are the mothers wha haena to bear,
Some time in their lives o' sic sorrow a share.

'Twas June, balmy June; the young laverock on high,
Carolled loud, and the merle essay'd a reply;
While the butterflee flutter'd among the wild flow'rs,
That grew roun' the door where the wean sat for 'oors.

The mignonette sweet, and the buttercups too,
On ilka leaf seem'd to hae keepit their dew,
To show fond affection, like tears in the e'e,
For Johnnie wha nursed them wi' self-conscious glee.

But sadness that morning had dimm'd the display,
Suggestive o' homage e'en Nature would pay,
For ere Sol the tap o' the Ochils had kiss'd,
The patter o' wee feet and sweet voice were miss'd.

When gently they bore her wee Johnnie awa',
Mony follow'd behind; blinds were drawn doon by a';
E'en wee Effie Gordon sobb'd sairly that day
For Johnnie wha wi' her sae often did play.

When the guidman cam' hame frae the dreary kirkyard,
Withoot speaking a word to the room he repair'd,
And there to his Maker he vow'd he would keep
The promise for his sake wha'd noo fa'n asleep.

As he slowly cam' ben she could easily see
The big tears o' sorrow well'd up in his e'e,
And the first words he spak were—" Oh, Ailie, tak' care
That ye put awa' carefu' this wee lock o' hair. "

He gied her the lock that he got frae the wean,
When he promised he'd never taste whisky again ;

" He tauld me, " quo' John, " that it was a great sin,
And drunkards to heaven would ne'er enter in.

" But sit ye doon, Ailie, " John tenderly said,
As owre to the chimla his dazed wife he led,
" And hear oot the on-gauns o' mony a year,
That's ruin'd and wreck'd me for life, noo, I fear.

" Sax years come this Christmas, a bonnie young bride,
Ye vow'd in the kirk that whate'er would betide,
Baith faithfu' and true until death to remain,
And tho' ye've had guid cause your love ne'er did wane.

" For a while a' gaed weel ; and when Johnnie was born,
A prooder man ne'er to his wark trudged that morn ;
And tho' 'tween oor cottage and smiddy there lay
Twa Scots miles, I'se hame aboot aicht times that day.

" Hoo my heart at that time turn'd as cauld as a stane,
Oh, Ailie, I doot I can never explain ;
Depression at times in a man's life ye'll find,
And sic to resist tak's a weel-balanced mind.

" When thro' at the smiddy, or dune playin' gowff,
We often adjourn'd to auld Nannie Wood's howff,
And there owre the yill stoup I ne'er thocht o' hame,
That o' a man's spare time the best part should claim.

"Then cam' weeks oot o' wark that sune ran into years,
Still I scorned the advice often gi'en in deep tears,
Till brocht to my senses ; was't God's ordained plan,
That a wean five years auld should chastise *a man ?*

"The orator's power, now I fain would beseech,
That erring Humanity's heart this might reach,
But oft sic has failed like the words o' a wife,
When a deein' wean's faith to a soul gied new life. "

He raise frae the chimla, syne fell on her neck,
And sabbit fu' sair wi' a heart like to break ;
She had to forgi'e him—what wife could dae less ?
He wasna the warst in the 'oor o' distress.

*   *   *   *   *

Mony years slippit by ; and baith geyan auld,
Sat patiently waiting His ca' to the fauld,
And often the twa, as they quately mused there,
Thocht on the langsyne and the wee lock o' hair.

But ae nicht at gloamin' when a' thing was quate,
The angel o' death stappit in at the gate,
And tauld them his message : " Prepared," they replied,
And gaed where nae trouble their souls can divide.

In the lanely kirkyard at the back o' the toon,
To the stranger wha happens to gang passing roun',
These words might be read on a simple heidstane—
" He keepit the promise he made to the wean."

—()—

JOCK.

CHORUS.

O but there's lear in Jock's pow,—
  A far-seeing callant, and couthy ;
He's set monie hearts in a lowe,
  And cares na altho' he's ca'd drouthy.

A DOUCE, buirdly fallow is Jock,
  I'm tauld he has plenty o' siller,
By clish-ma-clash Liberton folk,
  Wha lang kent his father, the miller.
Rob's gowd, when he dee'd, gaed to Johnnie,
And now he is bauthered by monie
  A kimmer, wha's reckoned by a'
Bien, blythsome, guid-natured, and bonnie.

He has acres o' ground, and twa coos
　　That romp in the field wi' the cuddy;
Cocks, hens, bubblyjocks, weel-creeshed soos,
　　And a frail, boo-backit auld body,
Wha keeps the " big hoose " for douce Johnnie;
　　She's no what you'd ca' awfu' bonnie,
　　But there lurks in the auld wifie's e'e
A something that fascinates onie!

The kimmers hae a' gane clean gyte,
　　Because the auld body's aye there yet;
They're jealous, and, ill-tongued wi' spite,
　　Say Jock and the wifie'll pair yet.
A' this has been whispered to Johnnie
By a sncevlin', decrepit auld cronie;
　　And they laugh owre the gill-stoup at nicht,
As they picture the sair hearts o' monie.

The gossips are seeking a clue,
　　Sae's to ken wha Jock's gaun to marry;
But that is a secret, I troo,
　　And queer are the stories they carry
Aboot the grand waddin' o' Johnnie,
And ferlie what gars him tak' onie
　　Auld body sae deaf, dottered, and frail,
When lassies there are young and bonnie.

The minister gaed doon the road,
    And twa o' the kimmers throughither
Sune speired at the guid man o' God,
    Quo' he wi' a smile—" Yon's Jock's *mither!* "
He rued what he said mair than onie,
For into his arms fell Kate Louie!
    Sic a gliff she ne'er gat in her life—
The wifie the *mither* o' Johnnie!

Jock married the lass he lang kent,
    Altho' monie fallows had socht her;
It wasna the presents he sent,
    Nor yet the fu' stockin' that bocht her.
The sense and guid nature o' Johnnie,
    Gar'd Mysie tak' him before onie;
And now Jock's mither relates wi' a smile
    How she in auld age deceived monie.

—o—

AT THE GRAVE OF KNOX.

I STOOD where he was laid—Elijah of his time—
    And noted " I. K. " on the simple stone,
And marvelled much if this be a neglectful crime
    Or honour to the Godly hero shown.—

Au honour, yea ; as heaven's glorious orb of light
  So will his name resplendent ever shine
  When graven stones as dust none can define.
So there alone I woo'd the silence of the night,
And weigh'd the mighty deeds accomplish'd for our sake
  By lion-hearted Knox, who fought the battle well
'Gainst anti-Christian foes, and worthily did make
  A roadway to the Christ, thro' carnal hell !
Thank God, the heavenly flame that burn'd within his
    soul,
The power of Rome could quench not, nor a nation's
    queen control !

—o—

JEANNIE.

Let Doric bards in dolefu' strain
    Lament the freaks o' Boreas,
And when blythe summer smiles again
    Their wood-notes wild throw o'er us.
Joy this to mony may impart,
    But sway'd by love,—life's dream,
The lassie wha has stown my heart
    Shall be the foremost theme.

The fond embrace I'll ne'er deny,
   Nor yet the sacred feeling ;
The throb o' love in ilka sigh
   Unconscious she's revealing.
Her bonnie mou' I aye maun pree,
   As Jeannie cares confide,
And tho' a tear may weet her e'e,
   Love's smile drives it aside.

Earth's star, protect,—O ! Thou, above—
   Wha frae my soul is never,
Whose constancy more true will prove
   Than the inconstant river,
For, oh, wi' winter's chilling breath,
   The water's flow may cease,
But no the love that outlives death,
   And gie's my life new lease.

—o—

ASPIRATIONS.

LONG I've striven to control
The emotions of my soul—
   In its ever fitful flight
To reach a higher goal,

Where a light,
Ever bright,
On the lofty hill of fame,
Lures me on, and I long
To immortalise my name
In a song.

In thus striving night and day
Do I idly throw away
What in solitude I prize?
No! a spirit seems to say
In soft sighs—
"O arise!
For vicissitudes of life
Ill to bear are below—
Labour nobly in the strife,
Soothing woe."

So, in trying to impart
Vital joy to every heart
I will emblaze with song
The glory of the art!—
Feeling strong,
In Life's throng;

And waking up my lyre
   With renewed delight,
I will in soul aspire—
   Still, to-night.

—o—

THE WEE ORPHAN LADDIE.

BAREFITIT and raggit, he hirples alang,
'Mang the rich and the poor on Life's roadway sae thrang,
And mony wi' tears in their een ye will meet,
At the sicht o' the orphan wha sings on the street.

Nae kind loving mother to ca' him her ain,
Or teach him fu' carefu' his bawbees to hain ;
He misses her sairly ; when rain fa's, or sleet,
I'm wae for the orphan wha sings on the street.

His claes are aye duddy, and as for his hair,
Frae Monday to Sunday the kaim's never there ;
When snaw's on the ground e'en a crust is a treat
To shriv'ring wee Bobby wha sings on the street.

Yet, aiblins, some day sune his struggles may cease ;
And when frae Life's burden Death gie's him release,
There's nane but the collie that oft licks his feet
Will miss the wee orphan wha sings on the street.

But, oh, while he's here mak' his burden fu' licht ;
Strive to guide the wee waif in the path that is richt,
And pray in your pity as a' your hearts beat—
God bless the wee orphan wha sings on the street.

—◡—

THE LAND WE LOVE.

THE land we love !—with pride I sing her dappled dells
  and knowes,
Where woodland burnies wimple, and the purple heather
  grows ;
The thistle, emblem o' the brave, blooms there owre
  cherished dead,
And on hillsides, immortal made, in grandeur rears its
  head !

Her grim, scarr'd, rugged mountains! ay, our hearts
    with joy may bound,
When history's page o' heroes tell wha rest there often
    found,
When footsore, worn, and wearied, frae the battle's
    bluidy fray,
Where they for Scotland's weal had focht in persecution's
    day.

They say the maids o' ither lands are gracefu' and
    divine,
We'll let them claim the laurels, but they never can
    ootshine
The rosy-cheekit lassies, wha sae blythe a-milking
    gang,
And charm the rural echoes wi' some guid auld
    Scottish sang.

The flowers o' ither countries may shed perfume thro'
    the air,
But wi' our bonnie blue-bells I canna them compare,
Or the gowans and forget-me-nots that deck the
    verdant lea—
The theme o' mony priceless sangs, auld Scotland's
    flowers for me.

Arise, ye poet preachers, and attune the deathless lyre,
To celebrate our rugged coast with grand poetic fire,
And toast—"May Peace and Plenty reign, while
    Worth and Valour shine,"
And aye uphaud auld Scotland's fame whose sun shall
    ne'er decline!

—o—

HENRY W. LONGFELLOW.

Born February 27, 1807. Died March 24, 1882.

A REQUIEM.

THE nations mourn! their gentle poet's dead!—
    Who strewed our pathway with undying flowers,
And by the life he ever humbly led,
    Portrayed the bliss that might by faith be ours!
No vain eulogium of tongue or pen
    Can e'er depict the glory of his lyre—
Now mute, alas! to be ne'er strung again
    Responsive to the Muse's sacred fire.

Not his to sing of sanguinary wars,
    Nor in heroic measure paint the field,

But rather to commune with night's lone stars,
    And aid what Science hath to us revealed.
The simpler and yet higher aims he sought
    To lay before the humble and the proud,
Shone out like sunbursts in the good they wrought,
    While fame proclaimed their influence aloud!

So when the evening of his life came round,
    And Death the reaper closed his glorious day,
The bard, prepared, reposed in faith profound,
    And thus his spirit calmly passed away!
Weep not! nor deem the poet dead—for thou
    Whose soul is bowed in sorrow's sanctity
May yet behold the patriarchal brow
    Of him whose dower is immortality!

—o—

THE COSY CHIMLA-LUG.

There's chiels wha aye stravaig aboot,
    And carena for their hame,
The comforts o' the chimla-lug,
    Whare burns love's sacred flame,

Within their hearts ne'er find a place—
 Fules! they micht aye be snug
When sitting wi' the wife and bairns
 Beside the chimla-lug.

When trauchlin' roun' aboot the toon
 Some folk whyles get a staw,
Wi' snares fu' mony, and the vice
 That soon wad taint us a',
For sic but tempts ye to defile—
 Ye may your shouthers shrug—
But peace and virtue aye ye'll find
 Beside the chimla-lug.

Wi' bairnies clinging roun' their knees
 Some folk can ne'er be fashed,
But gie to me heaven's pledge o' love
 When tidy and clean washed;
There's treasures in its sweet, sweet smile,
 When lying on the rug,
Losh! I delighted, sit and watch
 Beside the chimla-lug.

The cosy chimla-lug I loe,
 And aye I will maintain

There's nae place like the chimla-lug,
    Tho' it be e'er sae plain.
A proof ? 'tis said some beasts are wise—
    Let's tak' oor collie dowg,
You'll find when he is in the hoose,
    He's at the chimla-lug !

—()—

BURNS.

JANUARY 25, 1890.

BELOVED by all ! this day but closer brings
    Each throbbing heart to still sustain thy name,
And justly so, for in our wanderings,
    Where'er we may, progressive is thy fame.
Invested with such genius Scotland shines,
    And " brither Scots, " enriched, thy memory toast,
Nor wonder thou, for as the tendril twines,
    So doth thy songs, and fitly thus we boast.
Thy worth, O bard ! few fully comprehend,
    Nor realise the good thou doth create,

For this I claim—the heart is man's best friend,
  Not sordid wealth, nor lordliest estate !
And who so much that vital part hath swayed,
And Right since then in truer garb arrayed ?

—()—

STANZAS

On reading in the SCOTSMAN *John Stuart Blackie's letter
anent the seeming public apathy towards Scots song.*

> GUID save us a' ! is Robbie deid
> That Blackie maun pen sic a screed ?
> I'm unco laith to think, indeed,
>   That the Professor,
> Should tak' sic notions in his heid
>   An' turn transgressor.
>
> Has oor enthusiastic frien',
> Ance mair amang the mummies been,
> Or Celtic studies morn an' een,
>   Sae dreich an' kittle,

Cam' him an' common-sense atween,
      For, oh, he's little?

Or is he wi' Home Rule engross'd,
Like mony mair, wha, to their cost,
Noo count the hunners they hae lost
      Wi' sair distraction,
As owre the fire their taes they toast,
      An' wait re-action?

Na feth! John's never aff his feet—
Climbs hills, in fact, like Arthur Seat;
In spite o' snaw or scorchin' heat,
      Kail runt in hand,
He howks thro' ilk historic street,
      Baith steive an' grand.

That he sic nonsense should declare,
Wha's here an' there an' everywhere,
Wha, too, at socials tak's the chair,
      An' sae befittin';
Losh! by some mad dowg unaware,
      Is Blackie bitten?

Waes me! it's past a' comprehension,
Hoo sic rash statements claim attention;

Thro'oot the warld's wide dimension,
           Sair I regret,
This theory o' sang dissension,
           Micht tak' root yet.

What tho' his patriotic zeal,
West-End auld leddies canna feel,
And glaikit dochters skirl an' squeal
           High operatic;
Their lack o' sense they dae reveal,—
           Ay, maist emphatic !

What tho' the lords o' Moray Place—
Wha justice deal withoot disgrace—
Wad fain see his familiar face
           Within the dock,
An' thus revenge that injured race—
           The West-End folk.

What tho' they'd stop his waggin' tongue,
That often has their nerves unstrung,
Until wi' passion fairly dung
           Commandment three,
They whyles forget, an' swear that hung
           The fule should be !

To ither bards, if some gang fleein',
An' let's ken, too, that they've been precin',
That's no to say that oors are deein',
      Na, deil a bit ;
As lyric king—an' I'm no leein'—
      Rob aye will sit.

To sing Scots sangs a's no expected,
Sae think na then that they're neglected,
Ye wha owre sic micht be affected,
      Because a few,
Wham Labour has fu' hie erected,
      Keep shut their mou'.

We're no the least inclined to banish
Italian lays, or even Spanish ;
It's no the thing to be owre clandish,
      An' aye find faut,
For hasna ane whase bluid is Danish,
      A lesson taught ?

If Blackie wants us stirr'd anew,
Comparison he maun aloo,
'Twill dae mair guid—an' this is true—
      Than his lang screed.

Owre whilk, I'm thinkin', very few,
      Tak' tent wha read.

He'll maybe no admire my strain,
But feth ! oor sangs can stand their lane—
Nae clap-trap this—they will remain,
      The truth I'm speakin',
When in the yird his big heid-stane,
      Unborn are seekin' !

There's countless thousands nicht an' day,
Charmed wi' their sweet magnetic sway,
Sae wi' his havers haud away,
      An' ne'er mak' mention ;
It's infamy for him to play,
      For folk's attention.

Just let him practise what he'll preach,
Sae that the auld the young may teach,
An' editors their legs may stretch,
      Wha sit demented,
Oh, then I fervently beseech,
      He'll be contented !

Baith " Kelvingrove, " an' " Johnnie Cope, "
Stock pieces are—but why there stop ?

It is the country's earnest hope,
        He'll try the ithers,
E'en tho' dour critics on him drop,
        They'll please oor mithers !

In auld Scots sangs I've muckle faith,
To set them doon as deid I'm laith,
Na feth! for while her sons draw breath,
        Ye may be certain,
That there is naethin' but grim death,
        Will mak' a partin'.

Sae let oor sonneteering frien'
Put on guid specs, or rub his een,
An' he'll discover like a wheen,
        He's got nae gumption,
An' a' alang been unco green,
        Trick'd by assumption !

—o—

THE BONNIE LASS O' INVERARY.

OH, mony lassies hae I seen,
    But none, I trow, can equal Mary,
The bonnie lass wha cam' yestreen
    A' the gate frae Inverary.
The lowe o' luve both night and day,
    My heart has nursed a towmont nearly,
And now at ilka glance I hae,
    I seem to loe her mair sincerely.

My Mary's cheeks might shame the rose—
    The blushing rose, and oh, her eenie
Are jewels brighter far than those
    O' either Jessie, Nell, or Jeannie.
Her snaw-white teeth and ruby lips,
    Are just as tempting to her Johnnie,
As flowers are to the bee that sips
    Their fragrant sweets when blooming bonnie.

E'er Summer's smile forsakes the earth
   I mean to leave Auld Reekie's clamour,
And hie to her sae fu' o' mirth,
   For owre my heart she's cuist a glamour.
Through glens romantic then I'll stray,
   And speil Duniquoich's hill wi' Mary,
And view the scenes o' love's young day,
   When first we met in Inverary.

—()—

ROBERT FERGUSSON,

CANONGATE CHURCHYARD.

A FLOWER cull'd from the grave of one whose fate
   I mourn : nipt in its bloom, just like the bard
Whose dust lies here. I stand and gazing wait,
   As if he'd rise and eye me with regard.
Fergusson! immortal youth! how hard'
   And rough the road thou had'st to travel o'er ;
How soon, great light! thy genius bright was marr'd
   By Death, who led thee to another shore !
Some day, perchance, I musing here may stray,
   And place immortelles over thy loved dust,

And shed a tear, as I have done to-day :
  Fain would I linger yet, but ah ! I must
Depart in sadness as I think of thee,
Whose fate I mourn—which yet mine own may be.

—o—

TAMMAS STARK'S DRUCKEN WIFE.

Tak' tent a' ye wha tak' a drap,
  And aft into the yill-hoose stap ;
Come, hear ye this queer story oot,
I'se warn it's true, withoot a doot ;
Tak' tent, I say, frae what ye hear,
And dinna ghaists or bogles fear.

A sober chiel was Tammas Stark,
Baith late and early at his wark ;
In a' he did he socht the richt,
And tried to mak' his ingle bricht,
Tho' troubled wi' a randie wife,—
The plague and terror o' his life ;

A lazy guid-for-naething jaud,
Wha, when in drink, a' folk misca'd—
And sic a tongue! to match't we'd need
Big Peggy Stalker, lang syne deid!

At ither times Meg was fell dour,
And sulk'd and girn'd frae 'oor to 'oor;
Whyles she wad stacher up the stair,
And wi' a guid braid aith declare
That she, tho' seldom sober seen,
Ne'er drank in hiddlin's like a wheen!

Ae day Tam's wife was unco fou'—
A waesome sicht, ye weel may troo;
She pech't and sprauchl'd up the stair,
Wi' bauchl'd feet, and tousie hair;
Her shauchlin', shufflin', noisy din,
Brocht prying neebors ane by ane:
"Losh keep's! it's Meg Stark drunk again,
And canna speil the stair, tho' fain."
This roos'd Meg up, and to Kate Lloyd,
The wife wha spak' she thus replied—
"It's strange wi' me ye aye maun fash,
Ye sleckit, clish-ma-clashin' hash!
Gang ben and mind your ain fireside—

A pity but ye there wad bide ;
Ye blether sae 'boot ither folk,
Wha siller waste on drink and smoke,
But far waur things anent yersel',
Maist ilka ane can aiblins tell.
They say your rent is far ahint,
While aft your man o' meat ye stint;
Your claes and gear are in the pawn,
And a' the neebors roun' ye're awn ;
Tak' my advice, e'er ye complain
'Boot folk wi' fauts, scoore oot your ain !"

Kate, a' this time as quiet's a moose,
At length gaed ben into the hoose;
While neebors on the stair and street,
Held weel their sides for fear they'd spleet.

That vera nicht hame frae his wark,
At hauf-past six cam' Tammas Stark,
And saw a sicht that made him stare—
His wife lay deid drunk on the flair !
Quo' Tam, " I'll gie the jaud a fricht,
Before I sleep ae wink the nicht :"
And wi' a sigh o' deep despair,
He gaed straucht doon to Hugh M'Nair,

As Tam stapt into Hughie's hoose,
And saw baith man and wife sae crouse,
A short heart's-wish his lips did frame—
" Oh, wad to God I'd sic a hame ! "

Hugh's wife sat by the ingle-check,
Their bonnie wean play'd hide and seek,
Hughie, himsel', sat in the nook,
And on the table lay his book ;
A cheery fire burn'd in the grate,
Near whilk Tam took the proffer'd sate.
Nae words were needed to explain
The auld, auld story owre again ;
Sae Hugh gied counsel wi' the knack
To blend sic touches in the crack—
" A toom meal-pock will mak' Meg think,
And maybe, too, forsake the drink ; "
And sae a scheme was thus conceived,
That wad dae guid Tam Stark believed.

As twalve chim'd on the Tron Kirk nock,
The door-key grated in the lock,
And in there slade to Tam's hearthstane,
An eldritch wraith wi' waesome grane.
The sleeping baudrons fuft and glowered,

Syne as wi' common-sense empowered,
Lowpt into bed and claucht Meg's face—
(Long after't Tabby's scarts ye'd trace !)
Meg sprang attoure, and gied a skirl
That made the rafters a' to dirl,
For, wow ! she saw an unco sicht—
Nae wonner sair she swat wi' fricht.
A ghaist wi' face as white as death,
Sat on a kist in snaw-white claith !
Meg rubbed her een, gazed and wondered,
And aye the mair she was dumfoundered.
Wi' ootstretch'd haun's the figure raise,—
Whilk gar'd her een the mair to daize,
Syne slowly to the bed-stock slade,
And thus in hollow tones begade—
" I come frae regions doon below,
Whare ghaists and bogles glide in woe ;
Meg Stark, be warn'd in time, beware !
Gie owre the drink, or ill ye'll fare,
For Tammas Stark nae mair ye'll see,
As lang's ye tak' the barley-bree.
Sax weeks ye'll get your ways to mend—
Sax weeks, and syne your chance will end,
Then ye will maybe ca' to mind,
Tam, wha was aye sae guid and kind."

As Meg noo ettled to get up,
The ghaist a blanket up did whupp,
And flang't richt owre her heid and shouther,
Then vanish'd like a puff o' pouther.

Meg scream'd and cried baith lang and lood,
Until she saw a hauf-cled crood
O' neebor folk come rushing in,
Whase sympathy was " What a sin ; "
" Losh preserve's ! what is the maitter ? "
" Wha's sae abused the puir auld crature ? "
" A cryin' sin, it's past a' joke
To fricht the wuts oot harmless folk."

The wraith had sober'd Meggie weel,—
She hauflin's thocht she'd seen the deil ;
And tauld them hoo Auld Nick had come,
Syne vanish'd, she thocht, up the lum !

The auld wives gaped and cried "My conscience!"
While at sic superstitious nonsense
A hizzie to suppress her laugh,
Look'd up the lum, and thus got aff !
Meg trembling sat, and tears, too, shed,
Syne cannilie gaed back to bed.

For sax weeks Tam gaed whare nane kent,
'Twas then puir Meg did weel repent ;
She look'd sae pale, wi' chafts sae thin—
The vera banes shone thro' the skin !
When ask't to share the whiskey bottle,
She answer'd " No, I'm noo teetotal."
Oh, God, if folk this aye wad say,
When drink is put within their way,
I'm sure the wickedness on earth
Wad turn to virtue, joy and mirth.
Drink, cursed drink ! man's bitt'rest foe !
Parent o' murder, want and woe !
Help, brither man, the fiend to kill,
Whase victims work sae muckle ill ;
Ne'er put the bottle to your mooth,
And ye'll be happier far, in truth.
Bring helping hand and warm desire,
To raise the temperance banner higher,
Till a' shall worship at the shrine
O' water pure, the best o' wine.

Tam, honest chiel, is noo at hame,
Wi' smiling face and weel-filled wame ;
His wife's a pleasure noo to see,
As she sits pourin' oot the tea :

The hoose belike is greatly changed,
The plenishin' sae neatly ranged ;
The cups and saucers on the shelf,
Shine braw wi' ither pig and delf ;
E'en auld pot-lids upon the wa',
You'd tak' for mirrors, they're sae braw !

When Tam at nicht sits doon to tea,
His sonsy Meg's a sicht to see ;
Her cheery voice ilk ache and pain
Brocht on by toil can ease again ;
Yet whyles beside the ingle-cheek,
Fu' lang they'll sit afore they speak,
For visions are revealed at nicht,
O' clouded past and future bricht.

O ! happy change ! aye try thro' life
To keep in view Tam Stark's drunk wife.

—o—

WITHIN MY DEN.

'Tis midnight! yet before the flick'ring fire
 I sit with treasures priceless and sublime;
Men's mirror'd minds, that strengthen and inspire—
 Whose brilliancy illumes the realms of rhyme.

I read—and lo! in ecstasy am led
 Thro' " Nature's " glory, by the poet true,
Who grasp'd the lyre, and boldly thunder'd forth,
 Electrifying all, excell'd by few.
The air is fill'd with perfume of sweet flowers,
 I hear the warblers, and the babbling brook;
On all sides how transcendently portray'd,
 While genius glows with power.   Again I look;—

" Wee Jamie's chair" is close by " Nature's " side,
 I try, but cannot staunch the falling tears,—
The spring of feeling overflows so fast,
 Altho' it has been dry for many years.
And who is he that sketches thus so well?
 A genius great, whose arms have long been bare;

A prince of song, a navvy on the rail!
  World! think of it! and let thy great ones stare!

Here, by the good and gifted man of God,
  Who in life's happy-time did help to keep
My footsteps in their proper course, and thus
  The many tempting snares of youth o'erleap,
I " Raban " find, and mark it long and well,
  For who can e'er gainsay the limner hath
Succeeded not, nor soothed the soul perverse,
  And stemm'd the tide of discontent and wrath.

I turn me to " The Breeks o' Hodden Grey, "
  And see the men who wear them, swarthy, strong,
And high above the stir and noise I hear
  The anvil ringing forth its sturdy song.
A priceless dower!—his mission while on earth,
  To dignify our toiling sons in song,
Whose very life's-blood on their sweat-dyed brows
  Makes Labour march right manfully along!

" Burd Ailie " sitting dowie by the burn,
  Arrests my gaze, and moralising, I
Its pathos own a mental triumph vast,
  Tho' lowly hearths it may but glorify.

While in the distance " Ochil Idylls " rise,
    Like zephyrs sweet to cool the fevered brow
Of city men when Commerce jades the brain ;
    Than this, forsooth, what is more needed now ?

Now straths and glens, wild, bleak and desolate,
    Where waves the broom once dyed with righteous
        blood :
God's grace attend the patriotic Scot,
    High-soul'd and loved, for nobly he hath stood
Unflinchingly for Scotland's rights ; and tho'
    Years now fourscore hath pass'd, undimm'd
His genius, for with master-hand each day
    The " Highland Lays and Sonnets " still are limned.

Within my den are gather'd many more,
    By souls who sit upon the heights of fame !
Brave athletes ! who 'gainst fate have nobly fought
    And conquered. Blessed be the poet's name !

—o—

A COUNTRY IDYLL.

Wi' scented briar, and hawthorn here,
   What mair need I be wanting,
And yonder burnie wimpling clear,
   Thro' hermitage and planting ;
And eke Craigmillar's loved retreat,
   A sacred spot, and bonnie,
Where love, sweet rapture to the sweet,
   Reigns in the hearts o' mony.

Edina's sons, ne'er hang your heids,
   Nor let your cheeks turn blae,
But tak' the road ilk nicht that leads
   Where Nature holds the sway !
Where laverocks' songs and breath o' flowers
   Refresh the soul anew,
As doth the simmer morning showers
   That fa' as fresh as dew.

So let me hie frae Labour's din
 To some sequestered glade
Wi' Jeannie—gem my heart set in,
 And song-inspiring maid ;
Her charms I scarcely can define—
 A fairer flower ne'er grew,
And sweet as ony o' the Nine,
 That ever poet knew.

—o—

AN AULD WARL' WAIL.

" Losh ! " quo' my granny late ae nicht,
 As she sat by the ingle,
" I ferlie, Johnnie, gif it's richt
 For you to keep aye single,
For, 'od the lassocks, noo-a-days
 Are past my comprehension,
Wi' havers lang aboot their claes,
 A thing I ne'er did mention.

The papers I read ilka day,
 An' note the sad disasters ;

The hardships poor folk often hae
  Wi' tyranizing masters.
Nae wonder that I oft exclaim,
  'Hech surse! but this is awfu'!'
An', ferlie wha on earth's to blame,
  For it is mair than lawfu'.

The 'iron horse,' by some folk ca'd,
  Has lang been prais'd an' vaunted;
Noo, this is naething but a fraud,
  For it could weel be wanted!
The lives that's lost astonish me,
  An' yet folk doucely stand it;
Gif I'd my will, withoot a lee,
  I'd geyan soon disband it!

The 'Daphne,' that caused meikle tears,
  An' warl'-wide consternation,
Has drawn frae would-be engineers
  Mony a lang oration.
Frae this what guid will folk derive?
  Nane! but I hae been thinkin',
To dae withoot them gif we'd strive
  There would be less ship-sinkin'!

A birkie, too, ca'd Matthew Webb,
  Wi' meikle skill an' darin',
Life that is dearly prized lat ebb
  For nocht but fame to earn.
A foolish chiel he surely was,
  To work 'gainst God an' nature,
A' for the warl's lood applause—
  A maist ungodly feature.

Wi' fine persuasive airs a gowk,
  To me ae day cam' stappin';—
' A hole 'neath oor best street ye'd howk ? ' *
  Quo' I, 'That ne'er maun happen ;
Baith Scott, an' Allan, vandal rogue !
  Their sauls o' stane ye'd harrow,
An' mak' them envy Jamie Hogg,
  In peace beside the Yarrow ! '

In days langsyne sic freaks as they
  Were never hatched, I'll warrant ;
The folk then —this I'm proud to say—
  Were wise an' mair auld-farrant.
A quiet, peacefu' life a' led,
  Free frae inventive fever ;
Up wi' the lark an' soon to bed,
  Lang jinking Death the reiver ! "

* The proposed Princes Street tunnel.

A REVERIE.

I MUSING sit,
The earth is lit
With Luna's silv'ry light;
I see a star,
How bright, how far!
I dream of one to-night.

How pleasant thus
It is for us,
Poor toiling sons of men,
To sit and dream
By some sweet stream,
Or daisy-dappled glen.

Quietness prevails—
No sound assails
My ear, all now is hushed;

I muse on youth,
Hard times, forsooth,
Bright aspirations crushed.

But why repine?
A star doth shine
Resplendent night and day;
Where'er I go
My heart doth glow,
And Love supreme holds sway.

That star I own
As one alone
Who keeps me from all harm;
Her winning smile
Is free of guile;
Her voice it hath a charm.

Dear, beauteous star!
Oh, may nought mar
Thy prospects, now so bright;
May God above
Protect thee, love,
And keep thee in the right.

TO A BRITHER SCOT.

YOUR han', my frien', an' Doric brither,
Ye'll gie't I ken, withoot a swither;
In Glasgow toon there's no anither
   Like you, in fack,
Wi' wha I'd like, man, to forgather,
   An' hae a crack.

It warms my heart an' mak's it licht,
An' keeps tho bonds o' frien'ship ticht,
Lifting the soul aboon the blicht
   O' cauld despair,
That often sinks me day an' nicht
   Wi' heavy care.

I like your frien'ly way, dear Charlie,
For losh! man, I've ta'en to you fairly,
An' even noo I miss ye sairly;
   Mind, I'm no jokin',
Altho' I'm oot baith late an' early,
   At mony a rockin'.

But, heth, we'll meet again, I think—
Ay, mony a time, an' hae a drink,
Until—, a' richt, ye needna wink—
   I understaun'—
Ye gowk! nae wife wad gar me shrink,
   Nor even fawn!

I read your lines wi' muckle pleasure,
An' lang the sentiment I'll treasure,
Tho' justice in poetic measure,
   I scarce can dae
To ane wha sae adorns his leisure,
   An' sings away.

You say my muse, wi' ardour fired,
Has a' the gifts that are required
To soar, like ither bards inspired
   Wi' aim sublime;
Man! that's whare I hae aye aspired
   Frae early time.

I've socht a seat on famed Parnassus,
Beside the nine immortal lassies,
But hoo to gain it still harasses
   My burnin' brain;

Dool ! poets surely are but asses,
          Or else insane !

I fear 'twill end in Morningside—
A place whare I could scarcely bide ;
I'd rather jump into the Clyde,
          Or Firth o' Forth,
An' let my corpus wi' the tide,
          Be drifted North !

Then it micht float near han' Dundee,
An' lie ashore in state awee,
Whare fishermen would charge a fee
          To view the body,
O' " Laddie Bard, " noo drowned, ye see,
          Thro' rhyme an' toddy !

Meanwhile, accept o' this rough screed,
An' when the same ye chance to read,
Between the lines ye'll find decreed
          Still fond regard,
Sae wishin' you an' yours guid speed,
          The " Laddie Bard."

Postscript.

Man ! Charlie, I had maist forgot,
To say, yestreen, my heid gaed stot

Upon the grund, for, like a lot,
                    The cycling craze
Has nail'd me, sure as I'm a Scot,
                    An' changed my ways!

Sae dinna be surprised if soon
I tak' a run to Glasgow toon,
An' spend wi' you an' afternoon—
                    But haud your breath—
Frae aff my " bike " I micht come doon,
                    An' meet my death!

—o—

DUNNOTTAR.

DUNNOTTAR! once impregnable and grim,
    Confronts me now!—a skeleton of old!
    The longing wish that I might thus behold
It so, is realised :—from out the dim
    And doughty age, when king and men upstood,
    And fighting dyed the battlements with blood,
Where devastating Time still onward creeps ;

The wrathful sea, with spray-toss'd spotless hood,
    Around the dismal dungeons battle fierce!
For centuries meet dirge of restless mood
    And ceaseless wail. Gaunt ghost! still stay to pierce
The soul unpatriotic, for there sleeps
In yonder hallow'd moat, the martyr'd Scots who broke
Oppression's lance, so keen, and stifled bigots' croak.

—o—

OWRE THE FAEM.

" Fate has will'd, and we must part."

THE burnie sweetly sings its sang,
    The maukins frisk an' play;
But Ailie's heart gie's monie a twang,—
    It's fu', alack! o' wae.
The primrose that in spring appears,
    She heeds na noo ava',
An' bleart's her een wi' meikle tears,
    For Jamie, far awa'.

Oh, Ailie little thocht lang syne,
    When gazing on his face,
That thus the hamely muse o' mine
    For frien'ship-sake should place

A simple tribute, yet sincere,
　　To prove to ane an' a',
That still her laddie's heart is here,
　　Altho' he's far awa'.

His native hame he'll cherish mair
　　When faemy seas divide ;
An' in the braid Scots tongue declare,
　　Whatever may betide,
Auld Reekie, noblest to remain.
　　In sunshine, rain, or snaw—
A vision sweet, that haunts the brain,
　　In countries far awa'.

Like birds when nicht is near at haun',
　　I cease my song an' rest,
Yet know that ere the morrow's dawn
　　'Twill soothe a troubled breast.
In ither lands gin this he read,
　　It aiblins, may reca'
The chiel wha wishes him God-speed
　　Where'er his footsteps fa'.

—o—

DOUBT.

" Death levels all."

I STOOD within the solemn city of the dead,
  'Twas Autumn brown, and sear leaves thickly lay
Close to the margin of the lone and narrow bed
  Of her who nursed me in life's early day.
And as I stood, my wayward, trembling soul
  O'erflowed with grief, and filled my eyes with tears,
And in its sweep vile Doubt, that long held stern control,
  Destroyed, and inundated madd'ning fears.

Start not! for I had reckon'd death life's final goal—
  The great Beyond was fathomless to me,
But now in deepest sanctity my thirsting soul
  His power and mighty majesty could see.
And as I moved around I marvelled much that stone
  And sculptur'd pyramid should thus be rear'd
To wrestle with stern Time, and to the world make known
  Men's virtues, whom poor abject mortals fear'd.

Then saith I to myself, " Surely the mighty deeds
    Of kindness will outlive the stone, for hearts
Speak when Generosity rears its front, and seeds
    Of immortality spring from all parts."
So with a sickening sense I turn'd again, and sought
    The unmark'd spot where lay my love of old,
And bending low, I laid the immortelles I'd brought,
    Above the dust more precious far than gold.

And unobserved I knelt upon the clammy clod,
    The quiet seem'd my thirsting soul to fill
With deep contrition, and I sought the grace of God,
    Whom I had haply found at last, until
Dark ominous clouds athwart the heavens crept
    Like hideous phantoms, then I homeward turn'd,
Nor dreaded midnight's grim and lazy hours, but slept
    Untroubled, for the soul no longer mourn'd.

—o—

GOWFF.

(BY A NOVICE.)

THE cares o' wark confused my brain,
  An' feeling unco' dowff,
I thocht I'd ease the mental strain
  By gangin' in for gowff.

" A simpler game than this there's nocht,"
  Said I to Meg, my lassie ;
An' sae neist morn wi' pride I bocht
  A putter, cleek an' brassy.

Dark thunder-cluds the lift owre-cast,
  As doon the toon I hurried,
But what tho' win' was cast or wast,
  When I wi' " Rules " was flurried.

Ecstatic joy reign'd in my breist
  When on the links I stappit ;
An' tho' it rain'd, a round at least
  I'd hae afore I'd drap it.

A birkie, clad in gowfin' suit,
  Wi's blac, sair-drookit caddie,
Frae yont a dyke sat peerin' oot,
  Like some wild munelicht Paddy!

But sic I scorn'd! nae devotee
  Seeks shelter tho' it's rainin';
Besides, this gied the links to me—
  Long wish't-for luck I'se gainin'.

Frae aff my shouther gaed the clubs,
  For action noo prepared,
But clean bambazed, och! at the dubs
  I spell-bund stood an' stared.

Ay, horror!—mixed wi' deep remorse—
  Nae ba's I'd brocht! unlucky!
But rather noo than leave the course,
  I'd play it wi' a chuckie!

Wi' wistfu' mien I e'ed the dyke,
  For wi' the rain I'se soakit,
But shelter tak' I didna like,
  Sae to the gowfin' yokit!

The teein' grund I never socht,
  But doon the stane I set it,

My nerves at highest pitch noo wrocht
   To owre the bunker get it.

Alack-a-day ! ill luck, indeed !
   Nae wonder I did mutter
A smother'd aith, when swish ! the heid
   Gaed birlin' aff my putter !

Here for a month, as on a rack,
   I've lain up in the attics :—
Gowff's legacy ! a sair attack
   O' what is ca'd rheumatics !

—o—

ADELAIDE DETCHON.

QUEEN STREET HALL, EDINBURGH, DEC. 3, 1887.

COUSIN, adieu ! a fond adieu, for thou
   Within us hath created deathless claim !
Thou'rt forced, perchance, to cross the friendly sea,
Where others wait to wreathe anew thy brow,

And to their children's children hand thy name ;
But cherish'd memories must rise, and in thy reverie,
Undimm'd, Dunedin will remain, whose heart went
    out to thee.
When sour'd and sadden'd with the world's strife,
    Thine art, a potent spell, uplifts the soul,
For in " The Charcoal Man,"—a lesson strong
In all the stern realities of life—
    Our conscience conquer'd, owns thy vast control.
New love ! again farewell ! but let it be not long,
Until our hearts are thrill'd with matchless old Scots
    song.

—o—

ONLY A FACE.

ONLY a face, but a tale I could read
    In the hollow and pitiful eyes,
But oh, at what cost a moral it taught,
    Thus depicting the snares that arise.

Only a face, once as sweet as the rose—
    And her fate, too, like it,—bitter bane ;

Worshippers many while beauty did last,
   But when wither'd, they pass in disdain.

Only a face, with a wearisome look,
   That, alas! speaks too plainly of grief;
She pines for the grave, and knows well enough
   That her life here on earth will be brief.

Only a face, and a woman's it was,
   That one cold night I saw passing by;
It moved me I own; once pure she had been,
   And the pride of a fond mother's eye.

Only a face that would soon pass from earth,
   And forgotten, fade quickly away;
Wayfarer, alas! thou know'st full well
   The sad penalty frailty must pay.

Only a face, but this lesson it taught—
   Seek to know and perform what is right;
Vice, rampant stalks forth; be led not astray,
   But have faith in the Beacon of Light.

—o—

HOWGATE JOCK.

QUEER stories noo are gaun aroon'
Aboot the hairum-scairum loon,
Wha set the folk yont Logan Lee
As daft as honest folk could be.
A lazy, guid-for-naethin' tyke,
Wha late at nicht, ahint some dyke,
Wad sit for 'oors (nae fear had Jock),
Dress'd in his mither's muslin frock,
Wi' blacken'd face an' lang white bannet—
Cross-banes an' big green skulls owre-ran it !
An' a' to gie douce folk a fricht
Wha chanced to be oot late at nicht;
Jock ne'er was pleased unless aye bent
On some freak o' sly deevilment.

Weel, scarce a mile frae this fule's hoose,
There lived, on what he could produce,
A dour, ill-natured, girnin' body,
Ca'd Farmer Grieve, wha had a cuddy,

'Boot whilk at feein', tryst an' market,
Fu' mony to the tale hae harkit.

Some hare-brain'd chiel', wi' little sense,
Had got attour the farmer's fence,
An' ta'en Grieve's cuddy frae the shed,
Ae nicht when he was in his bed,
Syne put it in a field o' corn
That hadna jist as yet been shorn.
Next mornin', when Grieve heard aboot it,
He was at first inclined to doot it,
Until he saw the corn low laid,
That to him siller wad hae made ;
Then in a rantin' passion flew,
An' swore he'd mak' the villains rue
The trick they play'd that nicht, tho' he
Should swing for it upon a tree !

Sae, thinkin' owre't, as quate's a moose,
Next nicht auld Grieve slipt oot the hoose,
Roon' to the back to watch the door—
A thing he ne'er had dune afore.

An 'oor ootside he hadna sat,
When up he gat wi', " Eh ! what's that ?

It's fitsteps, surely, creepin' slow—
Noo is the chance to strike the blow!"
Dark was the nicht—ye scarce could see
At aicht yards aff, a hoose or tree;
But jist that meenit at his lug,
A man cam' by him wi' a dowg;
Sae Grieve turn'd roon' wi' boilin' bluid,
An' rush'd to whare the figure stuid,
An' gript him firmly by the throat—
But, by my feth! he met a Scot,
Wha there an' then did use his nieve
In spite o' cries for ae reprieve.

At length Grieve rose upon his feet,
As sair a sicht as ane could meet;
Syne gaed an' wauken'd up the hoose,
An' gar'd them let the watch-dowg loose.
To Tam an' Pate he gied command
To scoore the wuds wi' gun in hand,
Or wi' the dowg hunt doon the villain
Wha gied him sic a fearfu' millin'.

Sae aff they set for near a mile,
When they cam' slap against a stile
Whare gipsy tents were pitch'd aroon',

An' a' the gangrels sleepin' soun'!
But richt afore them, near a tree,
A form, wi' three dowgs they could see
Move on below the pale munelicht,
Like some dreid warlock o' the nicht ;
An' jist as they turn'd roon' to flee,
The dowgs rushed at them furiouslie,
An' wurried first the farmer's dowg,
An' chowed its jaws frae lug to lug,
Then set upon the ploughman, Pate,
An' bit him at an awfu' rate,
While Tam cried " Murder ! " whare he stuid
A' covered owre wi' dreepin' bluid.
This rous'd the gipsies frae their tents,
Wha gather'd roun' wi' fierce comments,
That werena vera nice to hear
To ony decent body's ear ;
While Tam an' Pate ta'en to their heels,
As if beset by howlin' deils,
An' sune got hame wi' ruefu' faces,
Their claes a' torn in shamefu' places.

A week gaed by ere girnin' Grieve
Could his ain ruif wi' safety leave ;

His nerves had been sae sairly shaken
That thochts o' **death** had left him quakin';
But sune as strength cam' back again,
Revengefu' plans burn'd in his brain.
Syne he gar'd Tammas dig a pit,
Near twa ell deep by thirteen fit
Or mair in length; an awfu' hole
To bury ony livin' soul!—
Jist richt fornent the widden shed
Whare the auld cuddy had its bed.
The trap was fill'd hauf fu' o' glaur,
To mak' the tummle a' the waur;
Saugh twigs an' grass the pit-mooth hid,
That nane micht ken—but them wha did.
Grieve chuckled owre the artfu' plan,
An' made cock-sure to catch his man;
But och! sic schemes "gang aft aglee,"
An' this did too, as you will see.

That nicht when Pate was in the toon,
He had a crack wi' Jock Colquhoun,
Aboot the trap that had been set,
An' three times warn'd him what he'd get
If gript,—but Jock jist only laughed,
An' said, " Ye surely think me daft!

Catch me ! my feth—as sure's a wuddy—
Instead o' me he'll trap his cuddy."
For be it kent, 'twas Jock Colquhoun
That frae auld Howgate had cam' doon,
An' ta'en the cuddy oot the shed
When folk were soun' asleep in bed.

Next mornin', near han' twa o'clock,
Grieve frae his sleep in fricht awoke,
On hearin' cries an' Wallace barkin';
He rais'd the winnock sash to harken',
When on his ear an awfu' bray
Was heard, like thunder far away ;—
" God ! that's the cuddy oot again—
I ken his roar—the thing's quite plain ; "
An' chucklin' as he thus withdrew,
He cried, " I hae the villain noo ;
Success at last has croon'd my plan,
An' feth ! I'll trap the guilty man ! "

Wi' dowg he set aff by the burn,
Jist whare it tak's a sudden turn
To brawl alang a darksome wood,
Whare ance a creakin' gibbet stood ;
An' there he's ta'en his eerie stan',
The dowg ahint, an' stick in han'—

A cudgel, feth! as thick's my arm,
Eneuch to dae the deevil harm;
When lo! before his glow'rin' een
A spectre on a beast was seen,
That gied his soul an awfu' fricht,
As on it cam' in braid munelicht,
A' dress'd in white, an' moving slow,
Like some appalling shade o' woe!
The farmer's senses seem'd to reel,
An' e'en his collie gied a squeal,
When aft wi' licht'nin' speed he flew,
An' then was heard a wild halloo;
The spectre followed het an' fast,
An' yell'd like murder in the blast,
Across the burn an' up the gate,
They drave alang, but ah! owre late—
The farmer an' the dowg an' a',
Ran richt against a ruin'd wa'!
Owre whilk Grieve loup'd like some gorilla—
The vera dowg seem'd made a fule o',
Then sprang attour his master's heid
An' scoor'd awa' wi' reekin' speed!
His master tummle't ance or twice,
Then up again jist in a trice,

An' made richt for the cuddy's shed—
The ghaist ahint whare'er he led;
Syne jist as he got to the pit,
A saughlin' twig tript up his fit,
An' owre he fell in his ain trap,
Wi' sic an awfu' yell an' slap,
As doon beside him, glaur'd an' muddy,
In rows his ain lang-luggit cuddy !

The servants roos'd wi' auld Grieve's cries,
To show a bold front ilk ane tries,
An' quickly jump frae oot their beds,
Wi' fear like what the guilty dreads
When death comes starin' in their face,
As hope forsakes their hopeless case;
Sae, rushin' oot at ilka door,
Like Bedlamites in some wild splore,
They ran to whare the noise was heard,
An' there, in truth, some monster stir'd—
Yet they could scarce believe their een,
That it was auld Rob Grieve they'd seen,
Until he roar'd, " What mak's ye wait ?
Come, help me oot this dreidfu' state; "
An' then wi' rakes they got him up,
An' drew him oot wi' nervous grup,

An' didna' fear to laugh ootricht,
When they saw Grieve in sic a plicht;
An' then they tried to save the cuddy,
Row'd up in something glaur'd an' duddy,
For it was covered wi' a sheet
That hung doon nearly to its feet.
A' this was dune by Jock Colquhoun,
The tricky, mischief-makin' loon,
Wha dress'd himsel' as weel in white,
Resolved to hae a nicht's delight
In hunting Grieve into his pit,
An' weel the rogue accomplished it;
Syne as he near'd the hidden snare,
The cunning fox ta'en every care
To leave the cuddy's back in time,
Tho' ane could scarcely see a stime,
Then pusht the brute richt in the hole
Whare Grieve knee-deep in mud did roll,
While Jock made aff wi' inward glee,
An' left them there to do or dee!

Next day the news spread a' aroon'
Hoo Grieve had been sae sair ta'en doon,
An' hoo his wife, near-han' dementit,
Fell in the pit owre him an' fentit!

The gossips roon' by Logan Lee—
A hantle mair than twa or three—
Long wonder'd wha had been aboot
That nicht, but it was ne'er fand oot—
For Howgate Jock, the slee an' bauld,
The secret ne'er to ony tauld.

—o—

BYGONE DAYS.

" Sublimely free ; where none intrudes,
I feel the trance of loneliness."

FROM labour's turmoil let me steal away
   To where the burnie smoothly glides along;
Half-hid by foliage from the glare of day,
   Where I may sing an unpretending song.
Sweet the release, as thus I roam with joy
Back to the haunts oft traversed when a boy ;
Light-hearted then, before dark grief and care
Oppress'd my soul with sadness and despair.

The village churchyard wears a peaceful look,
   So thitherward I slowly wend my way ;

How changed seems all since that last part I took
　In laying her in death's cold bed of clay.
Here undisturbed I raise the veil of years,
And see the maiden of my heart in tears!
We loved too fondly—but life's hopes were marred,
And now she sleeps within the old churchyard.

Time's ruthless hand hath many changes made:
　Now Commerce reigns where once sweet Nature
　　smiled;
The lover's haunt is now the seat of trade,
　Where sordid crowds resort with souls defiled.
Still old Craigmillar meets my ardent gaze,
And yonder fane revives the hymn of praise,
Where mother taught me early to adore—
O God! renew the dream of youth once more.

—o—

THE HAUDIN' O' THE BAIRN.

A DORIC DOMESTIC COMEDY.

"Sit doon an' haud the bairn, Jock, for oh, I'm tired
　an' sair;
There! gie it, man, that stick o' rock—its heid! losh
　keep's! tak' care!

Whaever saw the like o' that ? ye glaikit, senseless fule,
It's time, I'm thinkin', ye were at some oot-day nursin'
    schule !

" Ye canna haud the bairn ? o'dsake ! ye're jist like a'
    the men ;
Put on your braws, an' gang an' rake the streets till after
    ten.
What ! haud my tongue ? I'll no the nicht, unless you
    tak' the bairn,
An' let me gie my haun's a dicht, for I've the claes to
    airn.

" A bannet wi' a moss-rose flower, Jean, too's, been
    makin' up,
An' sae this nicht I maun rin owre, but losh ! your
    parritch sup."
" A' richt ! " quo' I ; " but dinna stey, for when his sicht
    ye leave
There's naethin' but a girnin' aye, that micht the hale
    land deave !

" You see as weel as me, guidwife, the bairn'll no keep
    quate ; "
Thae twa three simple words meant strife, (your ear, I
    dreided Kate !)

She took her shawl frae oot the kist, syne stapt to whaur
    I sat,

Dealt me a firm blow wi' her fist, an' cried, " Guidman,
    tak' that !

" Ye'll no begin your pranks wi' me ! na, feth ! I'll rule
    the hoose,

An' let folk see I'll rather gie than tak' frae you abuse.

Mind, here at nicht I'll hae nae strife, an' gin ye lift your
    haun',

I'll aiblins gie ye single life for sax weeks, understaun' ! "

Wi' that she left the hoose, an' clashed the door ahint
    her back,

The shock o' whilk aicht pictures smash'd, an' brocht
    doon, too, the rack

Whereon the delf sae showy stuid—delf she had kept
    for years ;

This I kenn'd weel wad raise her bluid, an' bring words
    to my ears.

I didna wait till she got hame but quickly gaed to
    bed

An' fell asleep ; when mornin' came she wauken'd me
    an' said—

" What gar'd ye lose your temper, Jock, an' smash the
delf like that ? "

But I ae single word ne'er spoke, altho' her een were
wat.

She noo saw plainly she'd been rash, but little guess'd
the door

Had been the cause o' a' the smash that still lay on the
floor ;

Kate thocht that I in passion strang, whene'er she had
gane oot,

Pu'd doon the pictures wi' a bang, an' flang the bowls
aboot.

Noo, I, in keeping to mysel' the rale facts o' the case,

Hae gied—an' I am proud to tell—dour Discontent, a
chase

Far frae the hoose whaur I reside in comfort wi' my
Kate,

Whase tongue at first I couldna bide—oh, wonderfu' is
Fate !

Noo, when my wife at nicht wants oot she doesna staun'
an' flyte,

Nor fling a bauchle nor a cloot like some ane gane clean
gyte,

But saftly tak's me roun' the neck an' says, " Gin ye're
no carein',
I'd like to see Jean Auchinleck ;   John, *dear*, ye'll haud
the bairn ! "

—o—

THE FISHER LASS.

CHORUS.

When breezes saft were blawin',
Ae nicht at gloamin' grey,
An' ploomen wha'd been sawin',
Did hameward tak' their way,
On Bervie Braes, a lassie fair
I met wi' bonnie gowden hair,
An' spak' her by the way.

THE lassies o' Auld Reekie toun
Are weel-faur'd, blythe, an' braw,
An' gin ye gang the warl' aroun'
Ye canna them owrethraw ;
But whiles, far frae life's bizzin' race,
A flower ye'll aiblins see

Whose modest, unassuming grace,
    Wi' ithers bears the gree.

A fisher lass o' low degree
    May hae a heart fu' leal,
Tho' lacking gear—a glancing e'e—
    An' rowth o' love as weel.
An' tent ye, tho' her humble hame
    The gaudy may pass by,
There's ane upon the saut sea faem
    Whase thocht's a' micht envie.

By auld Dunnottar's castled wa's
    Love's pledge at mirk is gi'en,
But ere another morning daws,
    Tears may start to the een.
But gin this fisher lassie wed
    The chiel wha gangs to sea,
May Fortune favours on her shed
    Where'er life's voyage be.

—o—

"NANA."

BY GOSPODIN MARCELL DE SUCHOROWSKY.

WHAT brilliant and consummate art is here revealed!
  A faultless form and face, whose liquid living eyes
  Prove far above the art's mere technique thou can'st
    rise.
O limner great! God spare thee long, that thou may'st
    wield
The brush, and Pygmalion-like, work into life
  By masterly manipulation such as this,
For sensuous passions universally are rife;
  But this ethereal and vivifying bliss
Makes earth a heaven, forsooth, and woman's worth
    ten-fold!
  Enthrall'd I gaze! and know not which most to
    admire,
Thyself or her whose lineaments confront me now?
To both I would bequeath the wreath that crowns thy
    brow.
  For did not Love and "Nana's" prototype inspire,
Till Genius, charmed at length, her aid could not
    withhold.

"ENGLISH AS SHE IS SPOKE."

"An almost incredible atrocity has been perpetrated in Glasgow. That home of English undefiled has been grievously insulted by a priggish educationist."—SCOTSMAN, SEPT. 16, 1886.

> *" Oh, wad some power the giftie gie us,*
> *To see oorsels as ithers see us."*

WAES me! St Mungo's in a plicht,
For wow! she's got an unco slicht,
Frae Education's august hicht,
   An unctious wail
Deservedly is brocht to licht,
   An' mak's a' quail.

Time there was when the mither tongue,
Was deftly woo'd by auld an' young,
But on your pride cauld water's flung,
   So tak' ye care;
Nae auld Scots sangs maun noo be sung,
   For poison's there!

The "mincing, mumbling" Glasgow folk,
Guid English jilt " as she is spoke,"
And doctor bodies greatly shock,
                    Wi' accent rough ;
Then comes the loud official croak—
                    A selfish puff;

" Until enunciation's clear,
The nursery's meet place I fear,
For jargon that assails the ear
                    At ilka stap ;
Contamination's gaun to bear
                    A fruitfu' crap ! "

To air this bauld pedantic view,
A whurly birkie starts up noo,
An' wi' remarks that arena true,
                    He tak's in haun',
To foist on us a Cockney stew—
                    Presumptuous spawn !

A weak-knee'd naig for you to ride,
Was Vanity, oh, Dr Clyde,
So stay ye at your ain fireside,
                    An' dry the cloak

That sank ye i' the surgin' tide
      O' wrathfu' folk ;

St Mungo, hang fu' laigh your heid,
An' frae a hank o' Jamie's threed,
Tie weel the tongue that does secede
      Frae accent pure,
Until in Cockney dress ye clead
      Your voice so soor !

—o—

LENORE.

OH, lovely, fair ; oh, lovely, fair,
  You move this heart of mine,
And bring to mind one as refined—
  Whom I adored langsyne.
Thy sweetness, too, revives anew
  The flame of love once more ;
And oh, thine eyes secure the ties
  That bound me to Lenore.

She sought in life to lessen strife,
  Where crime and folly reigned,

And overthrow the sin and woe
  Of Passion foully stained,
That thus the soul might own control—
  And seek God to adore;
Oh, yonder sun ne'er shone on one
  As good as my Lenore.

With winter came Death's silent claim—
  And shrined my saintly maid,
Whose acts of grace still find a place
  Where they will never fade.
And tho' the tears of bygone years
  Flow not; still, in my heart,
I proudly own, in thee, Unknown,
  I've found her counterpart.

—0—

FISHING IN THE TWEED,

THE ither morn wi' joy an' speed—for lang't had been
    my wish—
I set aff for the banks o' Tweed, wi' rod in han' to fish
Below the brig that half across puts you on English
    soil,
An' as I had nae time to loss I cuist my line for spoil.

The first twa 'oors the sun shone forth, an' sport was
    unco guid,
But soon a cauld win' frae the north began to freeze my
    bluid ;
However, up the Tweed I kept slow moving wi' my
    line,
An' into mony dubs aft stept, like Paddy Murphy's swine.

My hooks I'd soon hung in my hat, there is nae doubt,
    had I
No promised to the wifie that I'd bring her hame a fry ;

Sae no to mak' mysel' a fule, an' haud her scaulding
tongue,

I left the hame resolve to cool, an' "Caller Herring"
sung.

I just was at "Wha'll buy my ca—" when oot my
trembling han'

The rod was nearly pu'd awa'—wi' fricht I scarce could
stan'!

Guid save us a'! what can it be? quick—oot I swish'd
the line,

But owre my heid it gript a tree whilk some folk ca' a
pine.

Here was a fix! up soon I gaed, but quicker, feth! cam'
doon;

The only thing that made me fleyed was, had I split
my croon?

Wi' ae big lump upon my heid, I gat the line a' richt,

An' thocht I'd try ance mair the Tweed ere leaving for
the nicht.

In gaed the line! what—what is that? "By gosh!"
cried I, " a troot!"

An' fair owrecome wi' nerves I sat doon ere I'd draw it
oot;

But up at last, a' owre wi' sweat, thro' mony a thrawsome
    wauchle,
I landed safely at my feet a—what dae ye think?—
    a *bauchle !*

—o—

JAMES SMITH.

PRINTER-POET, AND STORY WRITER.

Born March 2, 1824. Died Dec. 12, 1887.

Gone from our midst! that manly heart of hearts,
    Whose unpretentious efforts lessons taught
    When deep-mind ministrations went for naught !
A player on Life's stage, whose many humble parts
    He play'd, and well. Adversity's most direful hour
    He felt ; but in its soul-refining power,
His Doric lyre, with nature's chords now strung,
Vibrated wheresoe'er was heard the Scottish tongue.
Create no sad regret ! hath Death claim'd all control ?
    A triumph over humble efforts done ?
    Ah ! surely not ; for as the glorious sun,
Uplifting in its daily course the sadden'd soul,
    So will Smith's songs a life's elixir prove
    Wherever human hearts fraternally may move.

JOHN BREMNAR.

(ON SEEING HIS PHOTO.)

JOHN BREMNAR! ay, assuredly this whim
With truthfulness brings back the sight of him
With lyart haffets, and the shrivelled form ;—
Who fear'd no man, and faced the wildest storm ;
Who grumbles not, but still with head erect,
Moves on and gains the burgh's deep respect,
  Describe John Bremnar ?—strange that's ne'er been
    done !—
Honest of purpose, face as sweet's the sun !
Sturdy and strong once, back now bent with years,
And broad brow bronzed and wrinkled ;—voice that
  cheers.
His old surtout's been thirty summers worn,
And truth to tell no part of it is torn ;
Antique ? undoubtedly, and meets the knee
Whereon the bairns are dandled—sight to see—
Young life and old in joyous ecstasy.

His pow is towzy, and his eyes ne'er lack
Deep sympathy ; voluminous his crack,
And connoisseur of quaintest bric-a-brac.
His wide-awake's familiar, and his " tile "
Has oft evoked the stranger's brightest smile ;
His wit and humour's ever crisp and keen,
Recalling what the bygone days have been.
Twice forty years life's ceaseless ebb and flow,
He's viewed, and strives even yet by acts to show
The noble mind triumphant will prevail,
Tho' flaunting Pomp and Arrogance assail.

    Such is John Bremnar, honest soul and true,
Whose outward semblance now confronts my view ;
Whose words and deeds are photographed to-day
In hearts, and generations yet may sway.

    True ! art as this must soon give way to dust,
But old John's worth will live in memory's trust.

—o—

TO HIS MEMORY.

ALFRED TENNYSON.

O HEARTS grief-stricken, irreparable thy loss!
  And nations bow in veneration for the dead—
  Great and illustrious. Across the bar hath sped
The high-soul'd Song God, shrined in immortality.
Not long the waves of knawing anguish deign'd to toss
    The aged barque whose treasures, no need now to
      presage,
    As the meridian sun, a glorious heritage.
His song of vestal purity and nobleness,
    Heart-throbb'd, illumes the dark recesses of the mind,
    And in the hazy labyrinth of Creeds combined,
The mysticism rent reveals Doubt's dull abyss.
Still'd now the voice? Nay, nay; all is not o'er and
    past,—
    The garland drops not from the Poet's brow who
      taught
Love, Faith profound, and Hope, that ages will outlast.

FINIS.

RHYMES FRAE THE CHIMLA-LUG.

By J. W. M'LAREN, "THE LADDIE BARD."

(Out of Print.)

Extracts from Opinions of the Press.

"There is unquestionable simplicity and freshness, both of mood and expression, in them, a flavour of very genuine humour, and a sprightliness of diction that is full of promise."—*Scotsman.*

"The appearance of such a book as 'Rhymes frae the Chimla-Lug,' agreeably reminds us that the spirit of Burns is not yet dead. These doric lucubrations show that their author, 'The Laddie Bard,' possesses in some degree the natural simplicity, the impulsive freshness, the genuine pathos, the exquisite humour of our national poet."—*Glasgow Herald.*

"Creditable not only to the 'Laddie,' but might almost be the productions of a much more mature poet. All the pieces have a purity of tone and refinement throughout which give an additional value to them."—*Daily Review.*

"His descriptions of nature are vivid and truthful, while he hits off the foibles and frailties of humanity with much humour and tenderness. The 'Rhymes' present features of interest surpassed by the lucubrations of few who have wooed the muse at his age."—*Edinburgh Evening News.*

"Highly creditable to the author. His homely, everyday pictures of humble life show a close observer of, and a keen sympathiser with, men in many of the passing incidents of their lives. The 'Rhymes' show that the 'Laddie Bard' has a good share of the poetic faculty, and with care and culture he will likely give the world something more enduring than the present volume, praiseworthy as it is."—*Dundee Courier and Argus.*

"The productions do the author great credit. To the lovers of the muse, 'Rhymes frae the Chimla-Lug' should be a welcome little treasure."—*Dumbarton Herald.*

"When we consider that the author of this little volume of poems and songs is yet a mere youth, being known chiefly as 'The Laddie Bard,' we are astonished at the amount of insight into human nature which the writer seems to possess, and of the happy gift of turning all around him into 'sweet flowing song.' We trust that the author may be spared to maturer years to add yet more to the songs of his country."—*Hawick Advertiser.*

"Wonderful specimens of precocious talent."—*West Lothian Courier.*

"The themes are all a hearty and healthy class, showing a creative imagination without much artificial polish. Poems which speak to the heart."—*Brechin Advertiser.*

"He depicts with much truthfulness, in Embro-Scotch, a variety of scenes at once life-like and humorous. His couplets run smoothly, while at no time does he sacrifice sense to sound. Humorous and pathetic by turns, a good moral strain runs through all his songs."—*Ardrossan Herald.*

"A youthful poet of no mean order. We wish for the volume an extensive circulation in token for the pains bestowed by the clever young author."—*Ratherglen Reformer.*

"A couthy casket."—*Scotsman (America).*

. . . . "Much enjoyment I have found in their perusal. You have struck the chord of nature. Go on and prosper."—*Rev. David Macrae, Dundee.*

. . . . "I have read enough of them already to form a very favourable opinion of their merits, and to appreciate the simple and sincere spirit in which they are written. I congratulate you on your success."—*Henry W. Longfellow.*

. . . . "Read many of them with pleasure. They are fuller of dialect than most Scottish poems, but interest me none the less on that account, while to your own countrymen they must have a flavour of nationality which will render them especially acceptable. I hope you will continue to find the flowery path of literature into which you have ventured more and more agreeable the further you wander in it."—*Oliver Wendell Holmes.*

𝕿𝖔𝖒𝖒𝖞 𝕮𝖆𝖙𝖈𝖍𝖎𝖗𝖔𝖓;

OR, PATCHES FRAE A PRINTER'S POUCH.

By J. W. M'LAREN.

Opinions of the Press.

"Mr. M'Laren gives abundant proofs in this publication that he possesses a rich fund of humour and a rare vocabulary of Scotch words, phrases, and idioms. Tommy's funny 'ploys' and escapades, in most of which his wife Tibbie takes a prominent if not a leading part, are described in a most amusing way. Most of the dozen articles which go to make up the tiny volume could be effectively used as 'Scotch Readings,' which have become somewhat fashionable in these times at festive entertainments."—*People's Journal.*

"We have derived much pleasure from the perusal of this book. The stories —which are twelve in number—describe the experiences of Tommy Catchiron and his better half Tibbie, and are very humorous. Mr. M'Laren is evidently a keen observer of human nature, and his pictures of the every day life of the lower classes are vivid and truthful."—*Scottish Nights.*

"Written in a spirit of broad humour."—*Literary World.*

"Mr. M'Laren has in this entertaining collection shown his ability to write prose as well as poetry. Tommy's experiences with Tibbie, the guidwife, are most amusing, and many of the readings might be found suitable for evening entertainments. The illustrations, which are comical in the extreme, give zest to the sketches."—*Hawick Advertiser.*

"This is a series of very humorous sketches in the Scotch dialect. It comes from the East whence is supposed to spring all erudition, and is a credit to its class of works. Mr. M'Laren does not, for the first time, court public favour; he has already won his laurels as a homely poet of no mean standing. His 'Rhymes frae the Chimley Lug' still ring in the public ear, and are still read round many a 'chimley.' Though he hails from the East, whose Scotch may not always be said to be classic, he has benefited so much by his acquaintance with west-country Scotch literature as to keep his pen clear of the many peculiarities that are to be found amongst oriental (Scotch) writers of the same class. His Scotch is, despite its nativity, decidedly Burnsonian, and therefore appeals more to us in the West. Mr. M'Laren's humour is of that knock-about kind which never fails to raise the laugh, and so graphic is he in his description, that his pictures are produced with a vividness worthy of a Flaubert or a Rabelais. The author has no mean power in setting off the salient points of a person's personality, and many a time one cannot help thinking that his characters are sketched from life, so realistic are they. In conversation he is quite at home, and many of his situations are not only very funny but highly dramatic. But you must read 'Tommy Catchiron' for yourself. Taken now and again it will while away many a morbid minute, and help to make a pleasant evening pass more pleasantly."—*The Chiel.*

"There is real humour in this little book, so readers, professional and amateur, should buy it."—*The Elocutionist.*

"The broad Doric humour of 'Tommy Catchiron' delineates Scottish home life in its humble aspects with rare fidelity. Though the fun is of a rollocking order, it is unmistakably natural, and is also distinguished by dramatic force and familiarity, which arrests attention, while the risibility of the reader follows the perusal of the sketches with refreshing zest. A healthy moral pervades the book and counteracts the levity of dramatic action."—*Dundee Weekly News.*

"These really racy and amusing sketches of the mishaps and adventures of an aged couple of 'Scottish Worthies,' by the author of 'Rhymes Frae the Chimla-Lug,' are worthy of a place beside 'Jeems Kaye,' or 'Tammas Bodkin.' It is a little publication that will not be loitered over, and it will afford many a hearty and healthy laugh. The author's Doric is generally pure, and such sketches as 'A Visit to the Waxwork,' 'Wannert in Lunnon,' 'The Hoosetakin,' and others we could mention, contain much genuine humour, as well as exquisite pathos, and touches that reveal a careful study of what is curious and droll in human nature. The most of the chapters are very suitable for public reading, and would take immensely."—*Brechin Advertiser.*

MR. GLADSTONE AND "TOMMY CATCHIRON."—"From a glance already taken I anticipate much entertainment on perusal. (Signed)—Yours faithful and obedient, W. E. Gladstone."